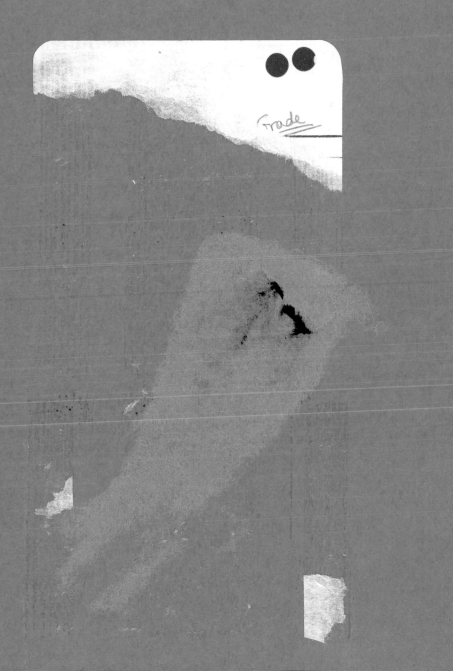

Grade

HERSHEL
OF OSTROPOL

By *Eric A. Kimmel*

Pictures by *Arthur Friedman*

The Jewish Publication Society of America   *Philadelphia 5741 / 1981*

Library of Congress Cataloging in Publication Data
Kimmel, Eric A.
  Hershel of Ostropol.
  Summary: Four stories about a clever man who lived by his wits
as his pockets were always empty.
  1. Ostropoler, Hershele,·18th cent.–Legends. 2. Tales, Jewish.
[1. Ostropoler, Hershele, 18th cent. 2. Folklore, Jewish]
I. Friedman, Arthur, 1935–. II. Title.
PZ8.1.K567He   398.2'2 [E]   81-6071
ISBN 0-8276-0192-1   AACR2

Designed by Adrianne Onderdonk Dudden

for Doris and Bridgett

CONTENTS

WHO WAS HERSHEL?

Hershel of Ostropol was a real person. He was born over two
hundred years ago in the Ukrainian village of Balta. But he
didn't stay in Balta, or anywhere else, for long. He spent most of
his life wandering from village to village in search of a living.

Most often, when Hershel wandered, his pockets were
empty. He had no money and no place to go. But since he was
leaving a village where he had no hope of finding work, Hershel
knew that his prospects in the next village could not be any
worse.

People who knew Hershel called him a "luftmensh." Luftmensh is Yiddish for "a man who lives on air." After all, if he didn't live on air, how else could Hershel survive without any money and without a job?

Hershel was no ordinary luftmensh. His sense of humor and his good sense kept him alive. The stories of his clever tricks and sayings have become so popular that, even though they all may not be true, they're still being told today.

WHAT HIS FATHER DID

One night, when Hershel was returning to Ostropol, he stopped at an inn along the side of the road.

"Please," he told the innkeeper, "give me something to eat. I've been walking all day and I'm terribly hungry. I'm so hungry, I could eat an elephant."

Neither the innkeeper nor his wife thought much of Hershel. "Don't be fooled," the wife warned her husband. "I've seen his kind before. He'll eat an elephant, all right. If we let him, he'll eat everything we have. But when the time comes to pay for his meal, he'll tell us he has no money. If he wants, let him sleep in the stable. But don't give him anything to eat."

"What will I tell him?"

"Tell him he came too late. Tell him dinner has been served and we have nothing left."

The innkeeper told Hershel just that. "I'm terribly sorry," he said. "We're all out of food."

"Not even a piece of bread?"

"No."

"A fishhead? A bone?"

"I'm sorry," the innkeeper said. "We have nothing."

Hershel's eyes flashed with anger. "If I don't get something to eat," he began very slowly, "if I don't get something to eat, I'll do what my father did."

The innkeeper was frightened. He backed away. Hershel grabbed him by the collar.

"Do you hear me?" Hershel shouted. "IF I DON'T GET SOMETHING TO EAT, I'LL DO WHAT MY FATHER DID! I'LL DO WHAT MY FATHER DID!"

The innkeeper ran to his wife in the kitchen.

"What do you suppose his father did?" the wife asked.

"What kind of question is that?" the innkeeper shouted. "Who knows what his father did? But whatever it was, his son will do it to us if we don't feed him. Hurry! Kill a goose and make him a supper. Give him the best food we have. Our lives depend on it!"

13

The innkeeper and his wife hurried. In no time a fine feast was spread on the table. Hershel's plate was piled high with food. Hershel ate it all. And whenever Hershel cleared his plate, the innkeeper and his wife served him more. Hershel ate until his buttons burst. He ate until he couldn't hold another bite. Ah, that Hershel could eat!

When Hershel was finished, when he couldn't eat another morsel, the innkeeper approached him timidly and asked, "Are you satisfied?"

"Am I satisfied?" Hershel replied. "I should say so! It was a wonderful meal. It was the best meal I ever had."

"Are you sure you don't want anything else?"

"No. Not another thing."

"Then you're not angry with me?"

"Me, angry? Forget it!"

"In that case," the innkeeper began. "I was wondering . . . would you mind telling me what your father did when he didn't get anything to eat?"

Hershel laughed. "Since you've been so kind to me, I'll be glad to tell you. At night, when my father didn't get anything to eat . . . he went to bed hungry!"

THE BANDIT

Hershel once went all the way to Borislav to borrow some money from a friend. It was a brisk autumn day just before Rosh Hashanah, the Jewish New Year. Hershel was returning to Ostropol when he decided to take a shortcut through the woods. He left the road and made his way through the tall, silent trees. Suddenly a bandit leaped out from behind a rock and pointed a gun at him.

"Your money or your life!" the bandit cried.

What could Hershel do? He handed over all his money. As the bandit turned to run off, Hershel spoke.

"Mr. Bandit, I don't care about the money. Keep it and be well. But could you do me one small favor? My wife doesn't trust me. If I come back without a scratch and tell her I was robbed, she won't believe me. She'll think I spent the money or lost it and made up a story about a bandit just to fool her."

"All right," said the bandit. "What can I do? How about if I give you a good knock on the head?"

"Oh, nothing like that," Hershel told him. "You don't have to hurt me. If you could just shoot a hole through my coat, I'm sure that would convince her."

The bandit told Hershel to hold out his coat. Then the bandit held up his pistol, pulled the trigger, and shot a bullet through Hershel's coat.

"How's that?" the bandit asked.

"Fine," said Hershel. "But perhaps one bullet hole isn't enough. Could you shoot another one here on the other side?"

The bandit cocked his pistol and shot a second hole through Hershel's coat.

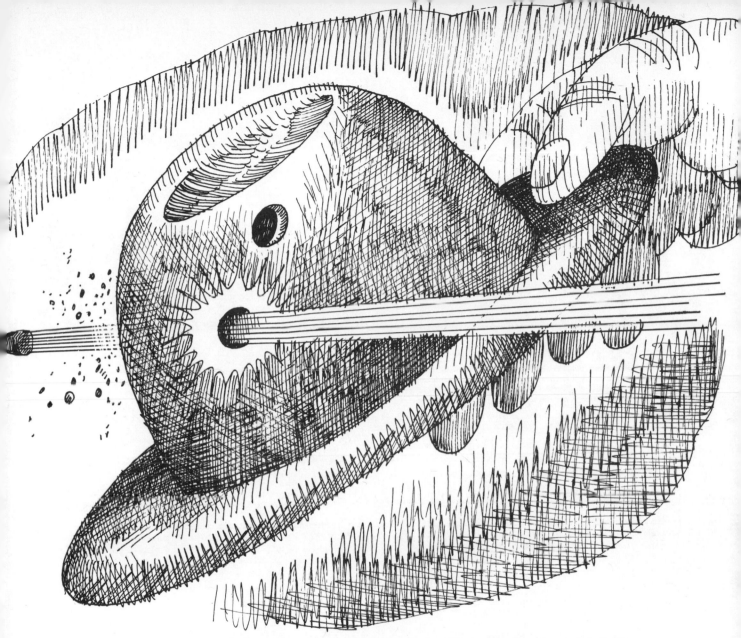

"A couple through my hat would really do the trick," Hershel said. He held his hat in the air while the bandit shot two holes in it.

"Now how about one more through my sleeve?"

"Sorry," the bandit said. "That's it. I have no more bullets."

"Not even one?" Hershel asked.

The bandit shook his head and showed Hershel the empty gun as proof.

"Well," Hershel said, "in that case I have something for you." He picked up a stick and hit the bandit over the head with it. Then, taking his money back from the robber, who was now lying on the ground, Hershel continued on his way home.

HERSHEL THINKS DEEP THOUGHTS

Hershel once had a job working as coachman for Baron Kowalski. Baron Kowalski was very rich, but he was also very stingy. He was known throughout the countryside as a cruel master who mistreated his servants, making them work hard for very little pay.

The Baron owned a stable of fine horses, which he dearly loved. In fact, people said he cared more about his horses than about his friends and family.

One day the Baron heard that several horses had been stolen from a nearby farm. He worried that his own horses might be next.

That evening the Baron went to the servants' quarters. "Hershel!" he yelled. "Sit outside my stable door. Keep your eyes open. There are horse thieves around, so don't you dare fall asleep tonight."

Hershel buttoned his ragged overcoat. He took a stool and went out to the stable. The Baron went up to his room and went to bed.

But the Baron couldn't sleep. He was worried about his horses.

"I can't trust that lazy Hershel," he thought. "I'll bet that right now he's fast asleep."

The Baron got out of bed, pulled on his coat and boots, and went out to the stables. There was Hershel sitting on his stool, bright-eyed and alert.

The Baron was pleased. "Well, well!" he said. "I under-estimated you, Hershel. I was afraid you might have fallen asleep."

"No, Baron," Hershel replied. "There's no danger of me falling asleep. I know a secret for keeping my eyes open."

"What secret is that?"

"I stay awake by thinking deep thoughts."

"Really?" said the Baron. "What sort of deep thoughts?"

"Right now," Hershel said, "I'm wondering what happens to the hole after you eat the bagel."

Baron Kowalski shook his head and went back to bed. But he still couldn't sleep.

"It's true that Hershel was awake when I checked, but I still can't trust him," the Baron said to himself. "He might think that since I checked on him once, he can go to sleep." The Baron thought about that a while. "I'd better check again," he told himself.

Once again the Baron pulled on his coat and boots and went out to the stable. Once again there was Hershel, eyes wide open, still sitting on his stool, still thinking deep thoughts.

"What are you thinking about now?" the Baron asked.

Hershel looked up. "I was wondering how a baby chick gets inside an egg."

"That's fine," said the Baron. "Go on wondering. Think all the deep thoughts you like. Just keep your eyes open."

The Baron went back to bed, but he still couldn't sleep.

"How can I trust my precious horses to such a nitwit?" the Baron wondered. He tossed and turned for an hour. Finally he pulled on his coat and boots and went out to the stables.

The Baron was pleased. There was Hershel, still awake, still sitting on the stool, still thinking his deep thoughts. Only this time the stable doors were wide open.

"Well," Baron Kowalski asked, "what deep thoughts are you wondering about now?"

"I was wondering," Hershel began. "I was wondering . . . what happened to the horses?"

A THOUSAND WORRIES

One day Hershel was walking by the river. He saw his friend Yekel the Coachman sitting on the bank looking very upset.

"Yekel, what's the matter?" Hershel asked, sitting down beside him.

"Oi, Hershel," Yekel sighed. "I have a thousand worries. My horse died, my coach is broken, there is no food in the house, my wife and children are wearing rags, the rent is due next week, and I don't have any money. What am I going to do? I have a thousand worries. A thousand more are on the way. I can't stand it anymore. I'm going to throw myself in the river."

"Yekel, Yekel," Hershel said, throwing his arms around his friend. "Things can't be so bad. We all have a little bad luck now and then, but it passes."

"Not when you have a thousand worries."

"You only think you have a thousand worries."

"What do you mean, 'think'? I do!"

"You don't," Hershel insisted. "I'll prove it." He took a pencil and paper from his pocket and began making a list.

"Let's see, a new horse costs how much?"

"Thirty rubles," said Yekel.

Hershel wrote down "30 rubles."

"Now how much to get the coach fixed?"

"Another thirty."

Hershel wrote down "30."

"New clothes for your wife and children—25 rubles. The rent—15 rubles." Hershel wrote it all down. "Now let's add it up. Thirty and thirty are sixty . . . and twenty-five makes eighty-five . . . and fifteen more makes an even hundred. Is that right?"

Yekel nodded.

"Then that proves it!" Hershel exclaimed. "You don't have a thousand worries. You have only one."

"What's that?" Yekel asked.

"Where are you going to get a hundred rubles?"

"So? Where?"

"That I don't know," Hershel said. "But I do know this. I don't have a hundred rubles either, but God always takes care of me. Have faith, Yekel. I'm sure He'll do the same for you."

And He did.

THE AUTHOR

Eric A. Kimmel lives in Portland, Oregon, where he is an associate professor of education at Portland State University. His previous books for children include *The Tartar's Sword, Mishka, Pishka & Fishka, Why Worry?* and *Nicanor's Gate.* His articles on children's books related to Jewish themes have appeared in *Response, The Horn Book,* and *Children's Literature in Education.*

THE ARTIST

Arthur Friedman's illustrations have appeared in textbooks, hundreds of films, and more than ninety issues of the popular children's magazine *Dynamite.* He is also the illustrator of *The Children of Chelm,* by David Adler.